A Mountain of Blintzes

BARBARA DIAMOND GOLDIN

ILLUSTRATED BY ANIK McGRORY

Gulliver Books
Harcourt, Inc.
San Diego   New York   London

In memory of my grandparents,
Rose and Joe, and Sarah and Harry,
who once upon a time ran a farm in the Catskills
—B. D. G.

For Mom and Dad
—A. M.

Library of Congress Cataloging-in-Publication Data
Goldin, Barbara Diamond.
A mountain of blintzes/by Barbara Diamond Goldin; illustrated by Anik McGrory.
p. cm.
Summary: A family works together to gather the necessary ingredients to make blintzes for Shavuot.
[1. Shavuot—Fiction. 2. Fasts and feasts—Judaism—Fiction. 3. Jews—United States—Fiction.
4. Family life—Fiction.] I. McGrory, Anik, ill. II. Title.
PZ7.G5674Mo 2001
[E]—dc21 00-8856 √
ISBN 0-15-201902-2

First edition
A C E G H F D B
Printed in Hong Kong

With thanks to Tali Edry and Esther Kosofsky, for their expertise and advice
—B. D. G.

The illustrations in this book were done in watercolors on Fabriano Artistico watercolor paper.
The display type was set in Artcraft.
The text type was set in Cloister Oldstyle.
Printed by South China Printing Company, Ltd., Hong Kong
This book was printed on totally chlorine-free Nymolla Matte Art paper.
Production supervision by Sandra Grebenar and Ginger Boyer
Designed by Lydia D'moch

AUTHOR'S NOTE

A Mountain of Blintzes is based loosely on a traditional Chelm, or Polish town of fools, story I first came across in *The Shavuot Anthology*, edited by Philip Goodman. I've changed the story quite a bit, setting it in the Catskill Mountains in the late 1920s, instead of in a shtetl in Eastern Europe in the 1880s. And I've added children who contribute to a happy ending. I chose the setting because, when he was a boy, my father lived on a farm in the Catskills, near White Lake, New York, with his two brothers, two sisters, and their parents, Sarah and Harry.

In researching this story, I came across several explanations of why blintzes and other dairy foods are eaten on Shavuot, the celebration of the giving of the Laws, the Torah, to Moses on Mount Sinai. Most important is the traditional likening of the Torah to milk and honey, as found in such biblical references as Psalms 119:103: "How pleasing is Your word to my palate, sweeter than honey," and in Song of Songs 4:11: "Honey and milk are under your tongue." Biblical commentators say these verses refer to the sweetness of the Torah, and they suggest acting them out by preparing foods made with milk and honey.

Whatever the reason, adults and children enjoy eating blintzes during this holiday— as do Sarah and Max, Moe, Bessie, Francie, Harry, and Natie in this story.

All year long, Sarah and Max worked hard. They fed the chickens, chopped the wood, planted the fields, and took in boarders to earn some extra money. Their children helped, too, but no matter what, Sarah and Max never seemed to have enough.

It was Moe, Sarah's oldest, who reminded her when Shavuot was but two weeks away. He was learning about it in Hebrew school.

"Such an important holiday!" said Sarah. "When Moses went to the top of the mountain to meet God and receive the Laws—such a meeting! Can you imagine?

"What a celebration we could have! What a mountain of blintzes I could make! If only there was a little extra to spare."

Sarah could just picture a big plate of stuffed pancakes. "I'll have to come up with a plan," she said.

Early the next day, Sarah thought of it. "Maxie!" she called. "I've been thinking about blintzes."

"You make the best!" he said wistfully.

"Not without buying the ingredients," Sarah said. Then she turned her purse upside down and shook it. Not a penny fell out. "But don't worry. I have a plan. You and I will do extra work."

"Extra! Who has time for *extra*?" Max repeated.

"It's only for two weeks," said Sarah. "Mr. Epstein needs help building those new bungalows and Mrs. Grossinger wants help with the washing.

"We'll put our earnings in the coin box every day," Sarah continued. "And soon we'll have enough for blintzes! You agree?"

Max shrugged. Did he have a choice?

"The Torah is sweet, the blintzes are sweet," Sarah sang that afternoon as she washed Mrs. Grossinger's sheets. She winked at Natie. "We have some blintzes to make—and soon."

"Blintzes, blintzes, a mountain of blintzes!" Natie chanted.

"Ach! What a boy! You remembered. A mountain of blintzes to make us think of the mountain Moses climbed. Up and down he went, to bring us the Torah, the Laws."

Sarah looked around. "So, *nu*, Natie. Where are the others? They should be home from school by now."

"Moe! Moe!" Sarah shouted into the yard and all the way to the woods. "Come help hang the laundry! Moe!"

There was no answer.

"Bessie!" Sarah called. "Francie! Harry! Where are you?"

Still no answer.

"*Nu?* Where is everyone? Just when I need help, the children disappear."

Later, after Sarah had collected her coins from Mrs. Grossinger, she stood all alone in the kitchen. Moe had finally come home and was doing his chores, with Natie tagging along. Who knew where the others were!

"If they aren't home soon, they'll be doing their chores in the dark!" Sarah grumbled.

Sarah was just about to drop her coins in the box when a brilliant idea hit her! *With Max putting in his money, there will certainly be enough for blintzes,* she thought. *He has more to spare than I do. I have to buy so many other things. There's candles for the holiday, and material to make the children new summer clothes.*

So Sarah, very pleased with herself, put her coins into her purse instead.

Max was heading home from Mr. Epstein's. The coins he had earned painting the bungalows jingled in his pocket.

He waved to Mrs. Katz, who was taking the cakes out of her bakery windows.

Then he stopped in Mr. Fitzgerald's grocery
to ask if he needed any more eggs to sell.

Up the hill and down the road, past the dairy and the Friedmans' house—and Max was home.

Max waved to Sarah, who was outside helping Moe stack wood for the stove. "What a wise wife I have," he said to himself as he went inside to put his coins into the box.

Max could almost smell those tasty blintzes. But he hesitated for a minute and was struck by an idea such as a genius might have!

With Sarah putting in her coins, we will surely have enough for the blintzes! he thought. *Sarah has much more to spare than I do. I have to buy wine for the holiday, and all the children need new shoes.*

So, Max, very pleased with himself, put his coins back into his pocket and went outside to help stack wood.

Every day the same thing happened. Sarah stood by the box, ready to drop her coins into the slot.

But then she thought of all the things she needed. She thought of Max dropping his coins in.

And each day she put her coins into her purse instead.

Every day when Max stood by the box, he thought of all the things *he* needed to buy. He imagined Sarah putting her coins in.

And each day he dropped his coins back into his pocket.

After supper one day, Sarah made the announcement. "It's time to open the coin box."

Moe, Bessie, Francie, Harry, Natie, and Max ran over to the counter where the box stood. Max had a dreamy look, as if when Sarah opened the box, a mountain of blintzes would cascade out, already cooked and sprinkled with sugar. Ready to eat.

Never had the house been so quiet. Sarah reached into her pocket for the key. Then she opened the lid and gasped. Max looked in and gasped, too. How could it be?

"Not a penny!" said Moe.

"You didn't put in any coins?" Sarah said, turning to Max. "Not even one?"

"And where are *your* coins?" Max replied. "Even one."

"I needed them," Sarah said. "I thought that with your coins, we would have enough for blintzes."

"And I needed mine," said Max. "I thought that with your coins, we would have enough."

Moe coughed.

Harry shuffled his feet.

Bessie and Francie giggled.

"*Giggles?*" said Max sternly. "This is not a time for giggling!"

"They're up to something," said Sarah.

"You remember how we've been so late coming home after school?" asked Bessie.

"I remember," said Sarah. "While Papa and I were doing extra."

"We were doing extra, too!" said Harry.

"I helped Mr. Fitzgerald in his grocery, for a sack of sugar," said Francie.

"Mrs. Katz gave me a bag of her very best flour, for sweeping her bakery," said Bessie.

"I promised to pick berries for Mrs. Friedman this summer," added Harry, "and she gave me three jars of her jam!"

"And I worked in Mr. Townsend's dairy and he's going to give me all the cottage cheese and sour cream we need," said Moe.

Sarah clapped. "Then we'll have our blintzes after all! See what smart children we have, Maxie?"

"Just like their parents!" Max beamed.

"Natie help?" said Natie.

"You'll help us make and *eat* the blintzes," said Sarah, and gave him a hug.

When Shavuot came, they had a mountain of blintzes with a mountain of other good things—candles and wine, not to mention new clothes and shoes for the children.

And Natie helped, spreading
jam on all the blintzes...and on
his face and fingers, too.

A Recipe for Your Own Mountain of Blintzes

This is the recipe my mother used when I was growing up. Because blintzes are fried, be sure to make these with an adult. —B. D. G.

Batter
3   large eggs, well beaten
½   teaspoon salt
¾   cup water
¾   cup flour

Filling (mixed together)
1   pound dry cottage cheese or
    drained regular cottage cheese
¾   tablespoon sugar
½   teaspoon cinnamon
¾   teaspoon vanilla
1   large egg
dash of salt

oil, margarine, or butter for frying
sour cream, jam, and cinnamon for topping

In a medium-sized bowl, combine eggs, salt, and water, and beat well. Gradually stir flour in until batter is smooth, with a syrupy consistency.

Grease a six-inch frying or crepe pan. Spoon in enough batter to make a thin pancake. Tip the pan from side to side to spread the batter. Cook both sides of the pancake over medium to high heat, until lightly browned all over. Turn the pancake out onto a clean dish towel or plate.

To fill the pancake, spoon a generous tablespoon of the cheese mixture onto the center. Fold in the sides and the ends, to make an "envelope" around the filling. Set aside. Continue making pancakes until all the batter and all the filling have been used.

Fry the filled blintzes in oil, margarine, or butter until they begin to brown.

To serve, stack the blintzes to look like a mountain on a serving plate. You can also sprinkle cinnamon in five little lines on the top of each blintz, so when two blintzes are placed side-by-side, they remind everyone of the tablets with the Ten Commandments, and of the holiday of Shavuot. Serve with sour cream and jam.

Makes 10 to 12 blintzes

Temple Israel

Minneapolis, Minnesota

```
         IN MEMORY OF
           IDA DEE
            FROM
        GRETA STRYKER
```